To JAMIE

Christmas 1994

To JAMIE

Christmas 1994

Anna Sewell was born in
Norfolk, England in 1820.

Her classic novel *Black Beauty*
was first published in 1877.

This edition published by
Coles, Canada
by arrangement with Brompton Books Corp

© 1994 Brompton Books Corp

Produced by
BROMPTON BOOKS CORP
15 Sherwood Place,
Greenwich, CT 06830,
USA

Directed by CND – Muriel Nathan-Deiller
Illustrated by Van Gool-Lefèvre-Loiseaux
Text adapted by Sarah Harris

ISBN 1 85469 872 9

Printed in Hong Kong

"VAN GOOL'S"

Black Beauty

Chapter 1
MY CHILDHOOD

My mother was called Duchess. The name suited her, for she was beautiful and elegant and very proud of her smooth, glossy coat. I don't mean to boast, but I was often told how alike we were. Although my coat is almost completely black, we were both thoroughbreds, unlike the clumsy colts I ran and played with in the meadows. Our master, Farmer Grey, was a good and kind man. "You'll be a fine beauty one day," he'd say to me, stroking the delicate white patch on my forehead. How long ago it seems, and how pleasant it is to remember. When I was young it seemed that everyone loved me, and I was always happy.

I have only one bad memory from those times. There would often be fox hunts across our fields, and it was terrible to see the poor foxes trying to escape. But on this particular day, something dreadful happened. One rider got over excited and forced his horse to jump a wide river. But the distance was too great, and the poor horse fell and broke his leg! The rider's leg was broken too, but a man's leg will mend. A horse's leg will never heal, and they suffer so much that they have to be put down.

Poor Farmer Grey had to carry out this task, and I saw that he had tears in his eyes. "Don't watch," my mother whispered. I turned my head, but I will never forget the sound of the gunshot as it rang out across the fields.

9

I always knew that one day I would have to leave the farm, for farmers raise colts to sell. That is how they make their living. "Don't worry," Farmer Grey would say to me, "I will find you a good master. And I am going to train you myself!"

Until then I had spent my time running freely with the other colts, racing across the meadows, and running to my mother for comfort when the huge, terrifying trains roared past. But now I was going to have to learn to pull a carriage, and to carry the weight of a rider on my back!

When Farmer Grey first put the horrible
metal bit between my teeth, I tried to kick
and run, and it took all his gentleness to
soothe me. Then came the bridle, fastened by
straps around my head and under my neck.
Next was the saddle, which buckled tightly
under my stomach. Worst of all were the
heavy iron horseshoes, nailed to my hooves.
But my master was kind and gentle, singing
to me softly to keep me calm. At the end of
each day he gave me sweet hay to eat.

Soon I could walk and trot and gallop
carrying him on my back, and I learnt to pull
a carriage, wearing a heavy harness and with
blinkers over my eyes to stop me looking
from side to side. He taught me well, and
soon the day came when he was ready to sell
me. Sadly I said goodbye to my mother and
to the only home I had ever known.

However, I soon forgot my old life for my new home, Birtwick Park, was beautiful. The house was set in elegant grounds, and my owners were pleased and happy to see me. Squire Gordon, my new master, was a well respected gentleman, although his manner could be a little stern. His wife fell in love with me at first sight! Unfortunately, it was plain to see that she would never ride me. She was too frail, and looked very thin and pale. But as soon as she saw me, her face lit up. "How beautiful you are!" she cried. She came forward and stroked my nose softly. "I have never seen such a deep black coat! We shall have to call you Black Beauty!"

"Black Beauty! Black Beauty!" cried their two little daughters and their son in delight, running to pat and caress me.

The Gordons owned two other horses. Merrylegs, the children's pony, was cheerful and friendly, but Ginger, a spirited chestnut mare, kicked out at me. "Be still, Ginger!" commanded John Manly, the groom. Gently but firmly he calmed her down. John's nephew, Joe Green, had just started as a stable boy. He was clumsy at first but none of us minded, for he was kind and loved us well. Ginger and I became friends, and as we trotted together in harness she told me how badly treated she had been. I realised then how lucky I had been to have such a kind master.

One day there was a terrible accident. I was harnessed alone to my master's carriage when we got caught in a violent storm. Squire Gordon was in a hurry to get home, as his wife would be worrying about him. "Black Beauty cannot go any faster, the road is too slippery," said John Manly, who was driving. The river had risen, and the bridge had nearly disappeared under the water.

"Don't panic," John Manly told me, "go on!" I trusted him, and took a few more steps. But when I came to the middle of the bridge I stopped again.

"Don't be scared, Beauty," said John Manly, urging me on. I was almost at the other side when disaster struck! The bridge collapsed under our feet and the carriage nearly fell into the water. Poor John plunged into the icy river but managed to keep hold of my reins. Seeing him struggle, Squire Gordon jumped in to help him. I don't know how I managed to reach the bank and pull them both out of the water. But I did! Wet and shivering, we made it back to Birtwick Park.

When we arrived, John hurried to change into dry clothes and told Joe to look after me. "Don't worry, Uncle," said Joe proudly. "I will take good care of Black Beauty!" He led me to the stable. My legs were trembling so much I could hardly stand. Joe rubbed me down carefully for I was hot and sweating. I really needed a blanket to keep the chill off, but because I seemed so warm he gave me a large bucket of water instead. I drank it thirstily, realising too late that it was the last thing I should have done. Within the hour I had a fever. Ginger saw me trembling from head to foot, and gave the alert by whinnying loudly.

John Manly came running. "Oh Joe, you fool!" he cried when he saw me. "You have given him cold water! And no blanket!" Little Joe stayed sadly by his uncle's side as he tended me, but I became deathly ill.

Over the next few days, Joe cared for me so lovingly that I slowly recovered. That's when I discovered how much I was loved at Birtwick Park. The first day Joe brought me out from the stable, the whole family was there to greet me, including Merrylegs and Ginger. The three children were delighted, and even the stern Squire Gordon stroked me lovingly. "You are very brave, Black Beauty," he said. But best of all, my beloved mistress was there. She was growing weaker and weaker, and hardly left the house. But that day she was determined to join the celebration. I will never forget her smile of joy when she saw me.

Chapter 3
GOODBYE, BIRTWICK PARK

Sadly, several days later, my mistress became much worse. Squire Gordon decided to take her to town to see the doctor. John and Joe harnessed Ginger and I to the finest carriage, then took their places side by side on the coachman's seat. Our masters settled themselves comfortably inside, and we set off. In town, Mr and Mrs Gordon were staying at a grand hotel, which provided large stables for their customers' horses.

While John and his nephew gave us our hay, a sullen-looking coachman prepared a stall for his horse. He smoked while he worked, and when he went out, I saw that he had forgotten his pipe. It lay, still smouldering, close to a pile of hay. At once I began to panic; whinnying and stamping. But John and Joe had seen nothing and left, grumbling at me for misbehaving.

Soon a fire was raging! I began to whinny and beat my hooves against the walls. As soon as Ginger and the other horses saw the flames, they did the same. Suddenly the door opened; it was Joe Green! The brave boy leapt towards me through the flames. He opened my box, and pushed me out. "Go quickly, Black Beauty! Don't be frightened!"

But the sight of the giant flames paralysed me with fear. Joe took off his scarf, and covered my eyes with it. As soon as I could no longer see the fire, I went out calmly. John met us at the door and led me away, soothing me gently. Ginger was still inside, and I whinnied as loudly as I could. She whinnied and stamped in response, and without hesitation Joe ran back into the inferno to fetch her. We were both saved! The other horses were not so lucky, and many perished in the fire.

But had the doctor saved our mistress? The next day, when her husband helped her into the carriage, she seemed weaker than ever. "The only way she will get well again," my master explained to John Manly, "is by living in a hot climate."

I did not immediately understand what this meant, but one morning, John harnessed Ginger and I to the big carriage, and drove the family to the station. Joe drove Merrylegs, who pulled the other carriage carrying the children and their nurse. When we arrived at the platform their trunks were loaded onto the train. It was only then that I realised our masters were leaving us forever!

"Goodbye, Black Beauty," said Mrs Gordon, "I pray your next masters will be kind to you."

"There is nothing to fear," said her husband, stroking me. "The Count of Wexmire loves horses." The family climbed into the wagon, and the frightening machine carried them away.

Chapter 4
EARLSHALL PARK

That same day, John Manly drove Merrylegs to the parsonage, where the vicar had promised to look after her. Joe took us to Earlshall Park, the home of the Count of Wexmire. We were greeted by his groom, York, whom I distrusted on sight. When he heard my name, he laughed out loud, and from that day on, he only ever called me, "that black horse."

When Joe tried to explain about Ginger, and how she needed to be treated gently, he sneered. "Highly strung is she?" he asked, scornfully. "She will soon have that knocked out of her."

"Be brave," whispered Joe as he left us, and turned away quickly so that I would not see his tears.

Our new masters were very rich and fashionable, and their great house was full of servants. Later that day, the Count and Countess came out to inspect their new horses. After studying us in silence, the Countess declared, "These horses are perfect, York, but they have no style! How would I look going out with such a pair? Shorten their reins!"

The fashion then was for tight reins which forced a horse to hold its head up. It looked very elegant, but the tight straps were painful and made it difficult to breathe. The Count tried to talk her out of it, but the Countess was determined. "Tighten them, York, tighten them!" she insisted. Although I could feel the strain at once, I stayed still. Ginger was trembling at my side, and I feared what she might do. Suddenly, just as the Countess was stepping into her carriage, Ginger reared up, kicking wildly. It took several servants to calm her.

33

After that, the Countess would have nothing to do with Ginger. However, her son was attracted by Ginger's rebellious nature, and took her for his own. He rode very badly, but at least she did not have to put up with the choking tight reins which I had to suffer. The Countess had taken a fancy to me, and liked to show me off to her friends, as if I were no more than a new clock or her latest hat. She even took me inside to paint my portrait! Day after day I would stand in her salon, trying to keep my balance on the slippery marble floor.

We were not the only ones who detested the Countess. One of the grooms, Reuben, hated her as well. Often while he groomed us he would mumble, "I am ashamed to work for such an idiot!" But despite his good heart, it was Reuben who was to hurt me. Because he was so miserable, he drank too much, and when he was drunk he could be thoughtless and cruel.

One evening when we were returning from town he stopped at an inn, and when he staggered out much later he was drunk. He did not notice when one of my shoes came loose, and I began to limp. I stopped in my tracks, but he beat me, snarling, "Go on, you donkey, we're late!"

I tried my best as he forced me to gallop over the rough road but soon my shoe came off completely. I lost my balance, and stumbled to my knees. With a groan of pain I rolled on to my side. The carriage jolted, and Reuben fell to the ground where he lay still.

It was morning before anyone came to find us. As soon as he regained consciousness, Reuben was fired. Luckily, I had not broken anything, and was looked after well enough. But as soon as the Count saw my damaged knees he declared to his groom, "Sell him! I only want perfect horses in my stable!"

More bad luck was to come, for that same week Ginger fell ill. It was Lord George's fault, for he had ridden her hard each day, and she was exhausted. The count decided to sell Ginger too, but sadly not to the same buyer. And so I lost my best friend.

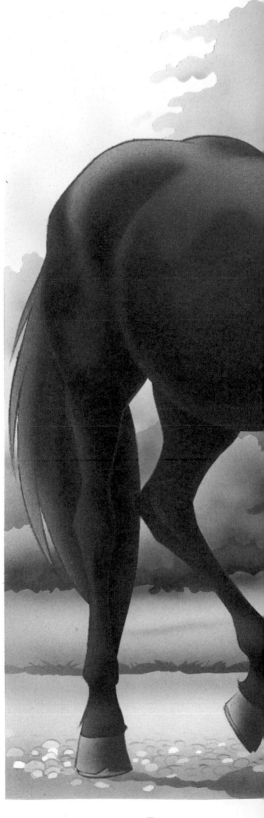

Chapter 5
THE LIVERY STABLES

My new master owned a livery stables, and hired out horses by the day. Each day I had a different master, and what masters they were! I am not saying that everyone who rented me to pull their carriage or to ride in the country was a monster, but none treated me as a living, feeling being. Because they had paid for me, they treated me like a machine. But the man I truly hated was the stable owner. He had eighteen horses and he knew how much we suffered, but his only concern was how much money we brought in. Every one of the eighteen horses hated him as much as I did. Of all the group, I was the gentlest, but it was I, Black Beauty, who one day reared up and kicked him! And kicked him so hard that he went flying across the stable and landed headfirst in the hay!

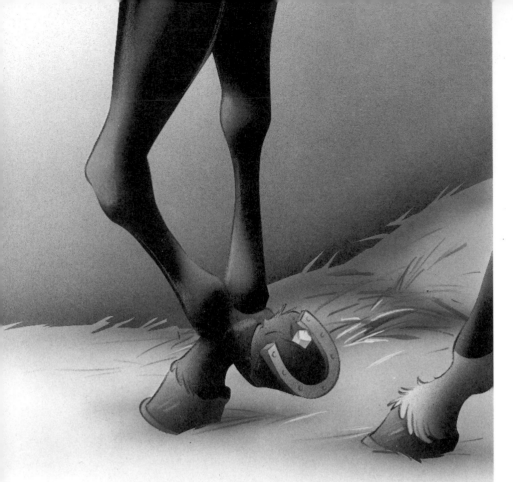

After that day, the owner deliberately rented me to the cruellest clients. The months passed. I was nothing more than a slave, to be beaten and whipped as he chose. Finally I was saved by an accident. One evening a stone lodged in my hoof and I fell to my knees. When I came limping into the stable, the owner cried, "You are no good for anything! I'd better sell you before you die!" And he took me to the horse fair.

For men a fair is an amusing event, but for horses it is humiliating and uncomfortable. Men stare at us, prod us all over and force our mouths open to examine our teeth. That day my knees were squeezed and poked so often that I whinnied in pain. The buyers jeered, "This horse can hardly stand!"

My owner insisted that it was nothing, that my limp would be gone in a couple of days, and that I was worth at least fifty pounds.

During this commotion I suddenly noticed a familiar face in the crowd. It was Joe Green! He wasn't a boy any more, but I recognised him at once. He passed close by without seeing me. If only I could whinny! But a buyer was holding my mouth open. Abruptly I pulled away, but it was too late – Joe had disappeared! The angry buyer stamped away, crying, "Your beast is vicious, keep him!" I was not disappointed that he did not buy me, for he was a brute.

Just then another man approached. This one was different. Immediately I knew that he liked horses. He stroked and patted me, then smiled at me, as if to say, "Do you think we two will get on?" I tried my best to make him understand that my answer would be yes. He could only afford twenty five pounds, and at first my owner was reluctant to sell, but when he realised he wasn't going to get a better offer for me, he gave in. Once again I had a new master!

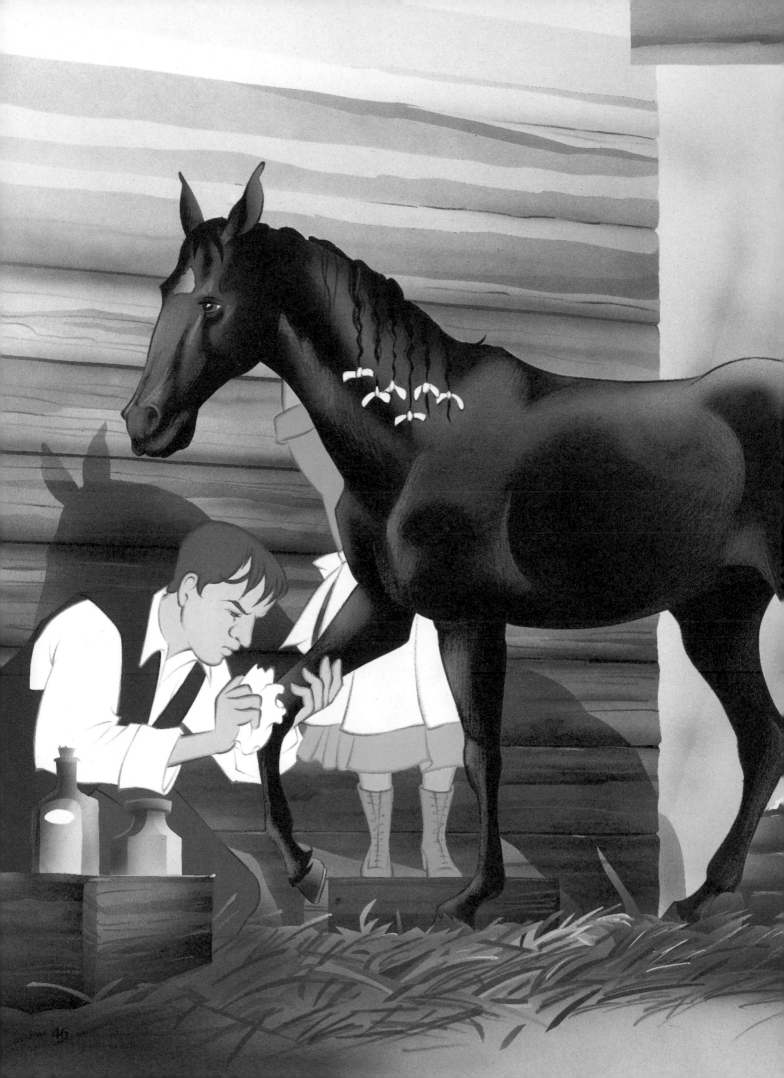

Chapter 6
JERRY BARKER

My new master was called Jerry Barker, and he lived in a shabby house in London. He also owned a tiny stable and a hackney cab. My new job was to be a cab horse! At first, the idea terrified me. But Mrs Barker and their two children were so kind to me that I began to calm down. Jerry tended to my knees gently, while his son spread clean hay in my stall. His little daughter put ribbons in my mane, and another on my tail. "You are very beautiful," she whispered to me. Their old horse, Jack, had recently died, and in memory of him they named me Black Jack. At last I had a name again, and half my real name at that!

While my legs healed, Jerry tried to gain my trust by singing softly in my ear. It was the same song that Farmer Grey used to sing, and it comforted me greatly. Once I could walk without limping, I had to brave the streets of London. How crowded it was! The noise was frightening and the smells suffocated a country bred horse like me! But I knew I was in good hands, and I went calmly wherever Jerry wanted me to go.

Customers were often in such a rush that they urged the cab drivers to push their horses as hard as they could. If there was a good tip offered, many of the drivers agreed and returned to the cab stand with a sweating, trembling horse. Jerry was poor, but not once would he consent to harm me for the sake of an extra shilling. "I'm sorry sir," he'd say, "but Black Jack is not a steam engine!"

Sunday was our only day of rest, but one Sunday Jerry agreed to take a customer into the country. A neighbour, Mrs Brown, wanted to visit her sick mother, and Jerry was so good hearted that he couldn't refuse. It was worth it to see how gladly Mrs Brown greeted her old mother. And while we waited to take her back to London we enjoyed a beautiful afternoon in the country. It was such a long time since I had run so freely, or eaten such fresh grass! Jerry sat and ate the lunch his wife had made him, feeding me sandwiches, and laughing at my high spirits. "Dinah Brown has promised to help me find a place as a groom in the country," Jerry said to his wife when we returned that evening. His wife laughed at him for being a dreamer, but she was glad for him all the same.

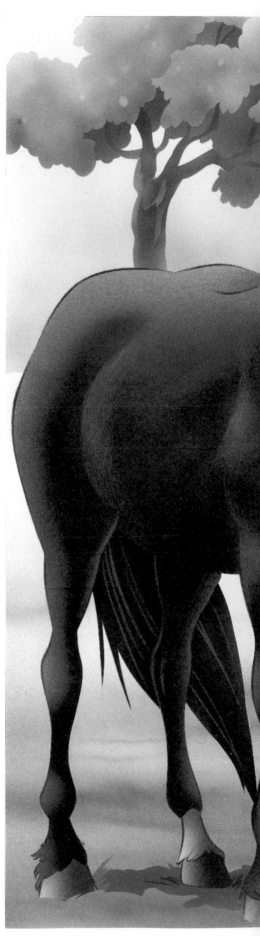

Chapter 7
THE WHITE PATCH

As the weather turned cold, life became very hard. London is a bleak and dismal place in the winter! It was then that I saw Ginger again. I noticed her one day in the street; she too had become a cab horse. But she had not had my good luck, for I immediately saw that her master treated her badly. He had worked her until she was exhausted, and no longer had the strength to rebel. She recognised me too, but as she began to slow down, her master flicked his whip and forced her to carry on.

Some weeks later, I saw Ginger for the last time. She was lying on a wagon, dead. Although I was very sad, I was glad that she had finally escaped her cruel master, and was suffering no more.

Winter is as hard for the cab drivers as it is for their horses. One night we waited in the snow for hours outside a grand hotel where our customers were playing cards. Jerry was worried about me. "How are you, my boy? Not too cold?" he asked, pulling my blanket up to my ears. But the next day it was Jerry who fell ill.

"It's serious," said the doctor. "If you want to get well, you must give up this job at once!"

Luckily for Jerry, Dinah Brown kept her promise and found him a place in the country; working in the stables. But he could not take me, for I was no longer handsome enough for a gentleman's stables. So Jerry sold me, despite the tears of his children.

"Don't cry, my dears," said my buyer. "I will take good care of him."

Once more I had to leave a family who loved me, and whom I loved. I tried not to show my sorrow, but it was very hard.

My new master did not keep his promise. He was a corn merchant and from morning to night he kept me pulling heavy loads, which strained my shoulders and made my legs wobble. I began to give up. He shouted at me, but I did not hear. He beat me with his whip, but I felt nothing. I had become a machine. I was like Ginger as she had been the last time I saw her alive. I cared about nothing.

Then one day, right in the middle of the road, I suddenly felt very weak. My legs gave way beneath me, and everything went black. "This is it," I thought. "I am dying. At last I shall be with Ginger!" But it was not to be. When I awoke, the furious merchant was standing over me. "You good for nothing brute!" he raged. "It is time to sell you!" These were his only words of comfort.

And so I made another trip to the horse fair. But this time I did not bother looking at what was going on around me. Head lowered, I dozed on my feet. Suddenly, a voice made me prick up my ears, a voice softer than any other – the voice of Joe Green! I opened my eyes and saw that he had already passed by without seeing me. But today no one was going to stop me from getting his attention. Gathering my feeble strength, I whinnied as hard as I could. Joe turned round. He was older and had grown a beard, but it was truly him. He came up to me, but did not recognise me. "What do you want, old boy?" he asked. Then suddenly, his eyes lit up. With a quick movement, he pushed back my mane, and saw my white patch! "Black Beauty!" he exclaimed. Taking my head in his hands, he stroked and patted me, laughing and crying at the same time. "Black Beauty," he repeated, "I can hardly believe it!"

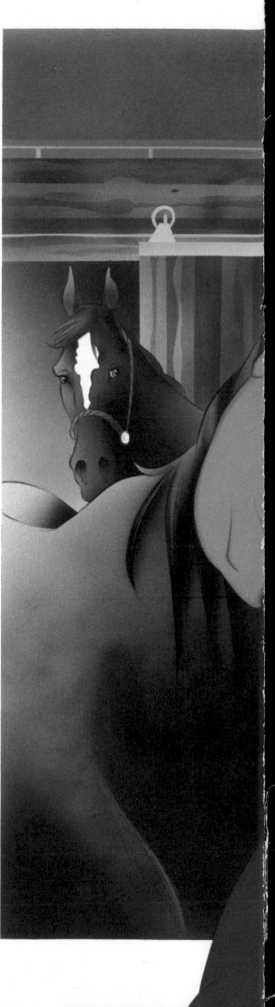

Now I live with Mr Thoroughgood, Joe Green's master, on a farm very like the one I grew up on. I play with the owner's little son, Willie, and sometimes I am harnessed to a light carriage, and driven by Mrs Thoroughgood and her friend Lavinia. This is the only work I do. I am loved and petted, and Joe looks after me well. With his good care and kind treatment, I have grown sleek and strong once more. And Joe has made me a promise. "No one will ever sell you again, Black Beauty," he told me. Who could ask for anything more?